The Frog Prince
and other stories
By
Walter Crane

The Frog Prince

Princess Belle-Etoile

Aladdin and the Wonderful Lamp

Introduction by Ruari McLean

MAYFLOWER BOOKS · NEW YORK CITY

First published by George Routledge 1874
First published in this edition 1980 by
MAYFLOWER BOOKS INC.
575 Lexington Avenue New York City 10022

Introduction © Ruari McLean

A Ruari McLean Book
in association with Mayflower Reprints

ISBN 0 8317 3665 8
LCC 80 - 83549

Printed and bound by
Van Leer & Company Limited, Holland

INTRODUCTION

Walter Crane (1845 – 1915) was an artist of many skills; but his 'Toy Books', of which three are collected in this volume, are certainly among the most beautiful picture books ever made for children. 'Toy Books' were paper-bound booklets, usually consisting of six or eight pages in colour and the same number in black-and-white, which began appearing in the early nineteenth century. To begin with, they were gay but fairly crude affairs, and their plates were usually hand-coloured. It was the wood-engraver and colour printer Edmund Evans who raised their standard and began printing the plates in colour. Evans was more than a printer who took orders from publishers: he actually commissioned many of the books he printed. It is to Evans that we owe the conception, as well as the execution, of that marvellous series of children's books designed first by Walter Crane, then by Randolph Caldecott, and then by Kate Greenaway.

Crane was just 18, and had completed five years apprenticeship to the wood-engraving firm of W.J. Linton, when he was introduced to Edmund Evans. Evans quickly recognized the young man's ability: "he was a genius" he wrote in his *Reminiscences*. Crane designed and drew about fifty Toy Books for Evans in about ten years. The first ones appeared in 1865 and although beautifully drawn were in a conventional mid-victorian style. In 1867, Crane tells us in his own Reminiscences, he was given a collection of Japanese prints by a naval officer recently returned from Japan, and suddenly – in the Toy Books published from about 1869 onwards – his style changed dramatically: it became more formalized, more decorative, more sophisticated, more original.

The three stories in this volume were all originally published in 1874. This was Crane's most mature period, when he was influenced by – and was himself an influence on – the so-called 'aesthetic movement' in London. His princesses tend to be of the Burne-Jones – Rossetti type, as are some of his compositions, especially in *Princess Belle-Etoile*: but individuality and humour keep breaking in, as in the frog drawings in *The Frog Prince*, and the various comic or grotesque figures that are always turning up (see the centre spread of *The Frog Prince*). The richness of colouring in these pages was obtained by Edmund Evans's use of no less than eight printings.

After about 1876, Crane stopped drawing Toy Books, and Edmund Evans, looking for someone to take his place in this field, found Randolph Caldecott. But Crane's influence remained strong. Kate Greenaway's decorative sense owed much to him; and many of Charles Robinson's illustrations for *A Child's Garden of Verses* (published in 1896 by John Lane, who was also republishing the Crane Toy Books) are very close to Crane. What a delightful book we might have had, if Crane had illustrated those classic poems himself.

Ruari McLean, Dollar 1980

THE FROG PRINCE.

IN the olden time, when wishing was having, there lived a King, whose daughters were all beautiful; but the youngest was so exceedingly beautiful that the Sun himself, although he saw her very often, was enchanted every time she came out into the sunshine.

Near the castle of this King was a large and gloomy forest, and in the midst stood an old lime-tree, beneath whose branches splashed a little fountain; so, whenever it was very hot, the King's youngest daughter ran off into this wood, and sat down by the side of this fountain; and, when she felt dull, would often divert herself by throwing a golden ball up in the air and catching it. And this was her favourite amusement.

Now, one day it happened, that this golden ball, when the King's daughter threw it into the air, did not fall down into her hand, but on the grass; and then it rolled past her into the fountain. The King's daughter followed the ball with her eyes, but it disappeared beneath the water, which was so deep that no one could see to the bottom. Then she began to lament, and to cry

when she again saw her beautiful plaything; and, taking it up, she ran off immediately. "Stop! stop!" cried the Frog; "take me with thee. I cannot run as thou canst." But all his croaking was useless; although it was loud enough, the King's daughter did not hear it, but, hastening home, soon forgot the poor Frog, who was obliged to leap back into the fountain.

The next day, when the King's daughter was sitting at table with her father and all his courtiers, and was eating from her own little golden plate, something was heard coming up the marble stairs, splish-splash, splish-splash; and when it arrived at the top, it knocked at the door, and a voice said, "Open the door, thou youngest daughter of the King!" So she rose and went to see who it was that called her; but when she opened the door and caught sight of the Frog, she shut it again with great vehemence, and sat down at the table, looking very pale. But the King perceived that her heart was beating violently, and asked her whether it were a giant who had come to fetch her away who stood at the door. "Oh, no!" answered she; "it is no giant, but an ugly Frog."

"What does the Frog want with you?" said the King.

"Oh, dear father, when I was sitting yesterday playing by the fountain, my golden ball fell into the water, and this Frog fetched it up again because I cried so much: but first, I must tell you, he pressed me so much, that I promised him he should be my companion. I never thought that he could come out of the water, but somehow he has jumped out, and now he wants to come in here."

At that moment there was another knock, and a voice said,—

> " King's daughter, youngest,
> Open the door.
> Hast thou forgotten
> Thy promises made
> At the fountain so clear
> 'Neath the lime-tree's shade?
> King's daughter, youngest,
> Open the door."

Then the King said, " What you have promised, that you must perform; go and let him in." So the King's daughter went and opened the door, and the Frog hopped in after her right up to her chair: and as soon as she was seated, the Frog said, " Take me up;" but she hesitated so long that at last the King ordered her to obey. And as soon as the Frog sat on the chair, he jumped on to the table, and said, " Now push thy plate near me, that we may eat together." And she did so, but as everyone saw, very unwillingly. The Frog seemed to relish his dinner much, but every bit that the King's daughter ate nearly choked her, till at last the Frog said, " I have satisfied my hunger and feel very tired ; wilt thou carry me upstairs now into thy chamber, and make thy bed ready that we may sleep together?" At this speech the King's daughter began to cry, for she was afraid of the cold Frog, and dared not touch him; and besides, he actually wanted to sleep in her own beautiful, clean bed.

But her tears only made the King very angry, and he said,

"He who helped you in the time of your trouble, must not now be despised!" So she took the Frog up with two fingers, and put him in a corner of her chamber. But as she lay in her bed, he crept up to it, and said, "I am so very tired that I shall sleep well; do take me up or I will tell thy father." This speech put the King's daughter in a terrible passion, and catching the Frog up, she threw him with all her strength against the wall, saying, "Now, will you be quiet, you ugly Frog?"

But as he fell he was changed from a frog into a handsome Prince with beautiful eyes, who, after a little while became, with her father's consent, her dear companion and betrothed. Then he told her how he had been transformed by an evil witch, and that no one but herself could have had the power to take him out of the fountain; and that on the morrow they would go together into his own kingdom.

The next morning, as soon as the sun rose, a carriage drawn by eight white horses, with ostrich feathers on their heads, and golden bridles, drove up to the door of the palace, and behind the carriage stood the trusty Henry, the servant of the young Prince. When his master was changed into a frog, trusty Henry had grieved so much that he had bound three iron bands round his heart, for fear it should break with grief and sorrow. But now that the carriage was ready to carry the young Prince to his own country, the faithful Henry helped in the bride and bridegroom, and placed himself in the seat behind, full of joy at his master's release. They had not proceeded far when the Prince heard a crack as if something had broken behind the carriage; so he put his head out of the window and asked Henry what was broken, and Henry answered, "It was not the carriage, my master, but a band which I bound round my heart when it was in such grief because you were changed into a frog."

Twice afterwards on the journey there was the same noise, and each time the Prince thought that it was some part of the carriage that had given way; but it was only the breaking of the bands which bound the heart of the trusty Henry, who was thenceforward free and happy.

PRINCESS BELLE-ETOILE.

ONCE upon a time there were three Princesses, named Roussette, Brunette, and Blondine, who lived in retirement with their mother, a Princess who had lost all her former grandeur. One day an old woman called and asked for a dinner, as this Princess was an excellent cook. After the meal was over, the old woman, who was a fairy, promised that their kindness should be rewarded, and immediately disappeared.

Shortly after, the King came that way, with his brother and the Lord Admiral. They were all so struck with the beauty of the three Princesses, that the King married the youngest, Blondine, his brother married Brunette, and the Lord Admiral married Roussette.

The good Fairy, who had brought all this about, also caused the young Queen Blondine to have three lovely children, two boys and a girl, out of whose hair fell fine jewels. Each had a brilliant star on the forehead, and a rich chain of gold around the neck. At the same time Brunette, her sister, gave birth to a handsome boy. Now the young Queen and Brunette were much attached to each other, but Roussette was jealous of both, and the old Queen, the King's mother, hated them. Brunette died soon after the birth of her son, and the King was absent on a warlike expedition, so Roussette joined the wicked old Queen in forming plans to injure Blondine. They ordered Feintise, the old Queen's waiting-woman, to strangle the Queen's three children and the son of Princess Brunette, and bury them secretly. But as she was about to execute this wicked order, she was so struck by their beauty, and the appearance of the sparkling stars on their foreheads, that she shrank from the deed.

So she had a boat brought round to the beach, and put the four babes, with some strings of jewels, into a cradle, which she placed in the boat, and then set it adrift. The boat was soon far out at sea. The waves rose, the rain poured in torrents, and the thunder roared. Feintise could not doubt that the boat would be swamped, and felt relieved by the thought that the poor little innocents would perish, for she would otherwise always be haunted by

the fear that something would occur to betray the share she had had in their preservation.

But the good Fairy protected them, and after floating at sea for seven days they were picked up by a Corsair. He was so struck by their beauty that he altered his course, and took them home to his wife, who had no children. She was transported with joy when he placed them in her hands. They admired together the wonderful stars, the chains of gold that could not be taken off their necks, and their long ringlets. Much greater was the woman's astonishment when she combed them, for at every instant there rolled out of their hair pearls, rubies, diamonds, and emeralds. She told her husband of it, who was not less surprised than herself.

"I am very tired," said he, "of a Corsair's life, and if the locks of those little children continue to supply us with such treasures, I will give up roaming the seas." The Corsair's wife, whose name was Corsine, was enchanted at this, and loved the four infants so much the more for it. She named the Princess, Belle-Etoile, her eldest brother, Petit-Soleil, the second, Heureux, and the son of Brunette, Cheri.

As they grew older, the Corsair applied himself seriously to their education, as he felt convinced there was some great mystery attached to their birth.

The Corsair and his wife had never told the story of the four children, who passed for their own. They were exceedingly united, but Prince Cheri entertained for Princess Belle-Etoile a greater affection than the other two. The moment she expressed a wish for anything, he would attempt even impossibilities to gratify her.

One day Belle-Etoile overheard the Corsair and his wife talking. "When I fell in with them," said the Corsair, "I saw nothing that could give me any idea of their birth." "I suspect," said Corsine, "that Cheri is not their brother, he has neither star nor neck-chain." Belle-Etoile immediately ran and told this to the three Princes, who resolved to speak to the Corsair and his wife, and ask them to let them set out to discover the secret of their birth. After some remonstrance they gained their consent. A beautiful vessel was prepared, and the young Princess and the three Princes set out. They determined to sail to the very spot where the Corsair had found them, and made preparations for a grand sacrifice to the fairies, for their protection and guidance. They were about to immolate a turtle-dove, but the Princess saved its life, and let it fly. At this moment a syren issued from the water, and said, "Cease your anxiety, let your vessel go where it will; land where it stops." The vessel now sailed more quickly. Suddenly they came in sight

of a city so beautiful that they were anxious their vessel should enter the port. Their wishes were accomplished; they landed, and the shore in a moment was crowded with people, who had observed the magnificence of their ship. They ran and told the King the news, and as the grand terrace of the Palace looked out upon the sea-shore, he speedily repaired thither. The Princes, hearing the people say, "There is the King," looked up, and made a profound obeisance. He looked earnestly at them, and was as much charmed by the Princess's beauty, as by the handsome mien of the young Princes. He ordered his equerry to offer them his protection, and everything that they might require.

The King was so interested about these four children, that he went into the chamber of the Queen, his mother, to tell her of the wonderful stars which shone upon their foreheads, and everything that he admired in them. She was thunderstruck at it, and was terribly afraid that Feintise had betrayed her, and sent her secretary to enquire about them. What he told her of their ages confirmed her suspicions. She sent for Feintise, and threatened to kill her. Feintise, half dead with terror, confessed all; but promised, if she spared her, that she would still find means to do away with them. The Queen was appeased; and, indeed, old Feintise did all she could for her own sake. Taking a guitar, she went and sat down opposite the Princess's window, and sang a song which Belle-Etoile thought so pretty that she invited her into her chamber. "My fair child," said Feintise, "Heaven has made you very lovely, but you yet want one thing—the dancing-water. If I had possessed it, you would not have seen a white hair upon my head, nor a wrinkle on my face. Alas! I knew this secret too late; my charms had already faded." "But where shall I find this dancing-water?" asked Belle-Etoile. "It is in the luminous forest," said Feintise. "You have three brothers; does not any one of them love you sufficiently to go and fetch some?" "My brothers all love me," said the Princess, "but there is one of them who would not refuse me anything." The perfidious old woman retired, delighted at having been so successful. The Princes, returning from the chase, found Belle-Etoile engrossed by the advice of Feintise. Her anxiety about it was so apparent, that Cheri, who thought of nothing but pleasing her, soon found out the cause of it, and, in spite of her entreaties, he mounted his white horse, and set out in search of the dancing-water. When supper-time arrived, and the Princess did not see her brother Cheri, she could neither eat nor drink; and desired he might be sought for everywhere, and sent messengers to find him and bring him back.

Cheri, that she fell dangerously ill ; and in the hopes of curing her, Petit-Soleil resolved to seek him.

But he too was swallowed up by the rock and fell into the great hall. The first person he saw was Cheri, but he could not speak to him ; and Prince Heureux, following soon after, met with the same fate as the other two.

When Feintise was aware that the third Prince was gone, she was exceedingly delighted at the success of her plan ; and when Belle-Etoile, inconsolable at finding not one of her brothers return, reproached herself for their loss, and resolved to follow them, she was quite overjoyed.

The Princess was disguised as a cavalier, but had no other armour than her helmet. She was dreadfully cold as she drew near the rock, but seeing a turtle-dove lying on the snow, she took it up, warmed it, and restored it to life : and the dove reviving, gaily said, " I know you, in spite of your disguise ; follow my advice : when you arrive at the rock, remain at the bottom and begin to sing the sweetest song you know ; the green bird will listen to you ; you must then pretend to go to sleep ; when it sees me, it will come down to peck me, and at that moment you will be able to seize it."

All this fell out as the Dove foretold. The green bird begged for liberty. " First," said Belle-Etoile, " I wish that thou wouldst restore my three brothers to me."

" Under my left wing there is a red feather," said the bird : " pull it out, and touch the rock with it."

The Princess hastened to do as she was instructed ; the rock split from the top to the bottom : she entered with a victorious air the hall in which stood the three Princes with many others ; she ran towards Cheri, who did not know her in her helmet and male attire, and could neither speak nor move. The green bird then told the Princess she must rub the eyes and mouth of all those she wished to disenchant with the red feather, which good office she did to all.

The three Princes and Belle-Etoile hastened to present themselves to the King ; and when Belle-Etoile showed her treasures, the little green bird told him that the Princes Petit-Soleil and Heureux and the Princess Belle-Etoile were his children, and that Prince Cheri was his nephew. Queen Blondine, who had mourned for them all these years, embraced them, and the wicked Queen-Mother and old Feintise were justly punished. And the King, who thought his nephew Cheri the handsomest man at Court, consented to his marriage with Belle-Etoile. And lastly, to make everyone happy, the King sent for the Corsair and his wife, who gladly came.

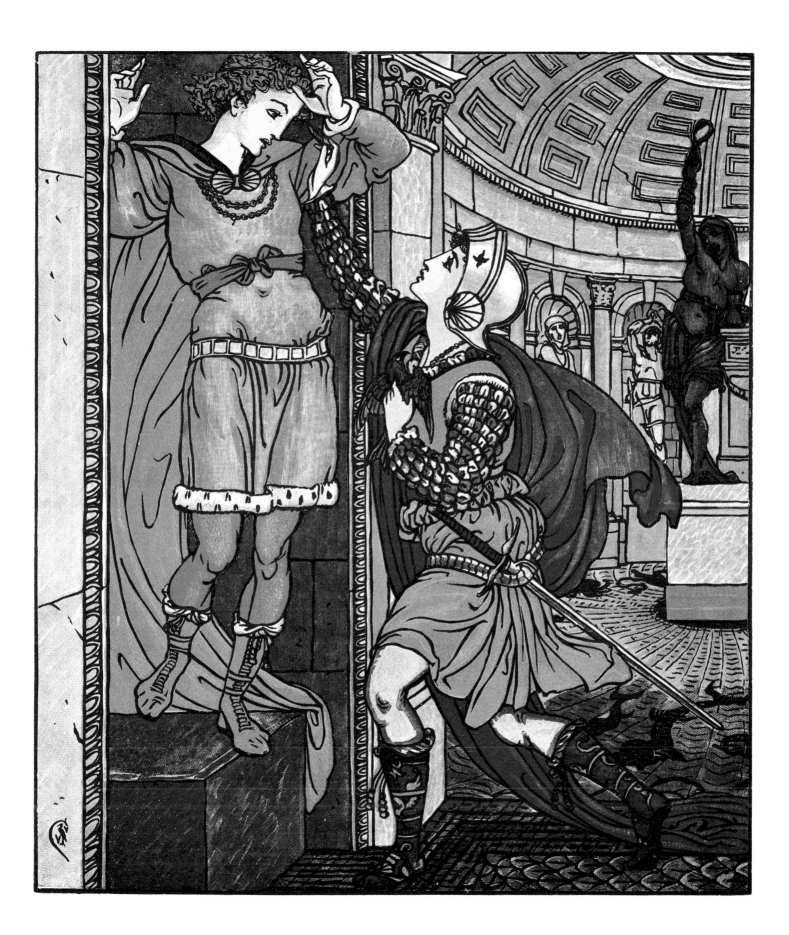

ALADDIN,

AND THE WONDERFUL LAMP.

ALADDIN was the son of a poor tailor in an
Eastern city. He was a spoiled boy, and loved
play better than work; so that when Mustapha,
his father, died, he was not able to earn his living;
and his poor mother had to spin cotton all day
long to procure food for their support. But she
dearly loved her son, knowing that he had a good
heart, and she believed that as he grew older he
would do better, and become at last a worthy and
prosperous man. One day, when Aladdin was
walking outside the town, an old man came up to
him, and looking very hard in his face, said he was
his father's brother, and had long been away in a
distant country, but that now he wished to help his
nephew to get on. He then put a ring on the
boy's finger, telling him that no harm could happen
to him so long as he wore it. Now, this strange
man was no uncle of Aladdin, nor was he related

at all to him; but he was a wicked magician, who wanted to make use of the lad's services, as we shall see presently.

The old man led Aladdin a good way into the country, until they came to a very lonely spot between two lofty black mountains. Here he lighted a fire, and threw into it some gum, all the time repeating many strange words. The ground then opened just before them, and a stone trap-door appeared. After lifting this up, the Magician told Aladdin to go below, down some broken steps, and at the foot of these he would find three halls, in the last of which was a door leading to a garden full of beautiful trees; this he was to cross, and after mounting some more steps, he would come to a terrace, when he would see a niche, in which there was a lighted Lamp. He was then to take the Lamp, put out the light, empty the oil, and bring it away with him.

Aladdin found all the Magician had told him to be true; he passed quickly but cautiously through the three halls, so as not even to touch the walls with his clothes, as the Magician had directed. He took the Lamp from the niche, threw out the oil, and put it in his bosom. As he came back through the garden, his eyes were dazzled with the bright-coloured fruits on the trees, shining

like glass. Many of these he plucked and put in his pockets, and then returned with the Lamp, and called upon his uncle to help him up the broken steps. "Give me the Lamp," said the old man, angrily. "Not till I get out safe," cried the boy. The Magician, in a passion, then slammed down the trap-door, and Aladdin was shut up fast enough. While crying bitterly, he by chance rubbed the ring, and a figure appeared before him, saying, " I am your slave, the Genius of the Ring; what do you desire?"

Aladdin told the Genius of the Ring that he only wanted to be set free, and to be taken back to his mother. In an instant he found himself at home, very hungry, and his poor mother was much pleased to see him again. He told her all that had happened; she then felt curious to look at the Lamp he had brought, and began rubbing it, to make it shine brighter. Both were quite amazed at seeing rise before them a strange figure; this proved to be the Genius of the Lamp, who asked for their commands. On hearing that food was what they most wanted, a black slave instantly entered with the choicest fare upon a dainty dish of silver, and with silver plates for them to eat from.

Aladdin and his mother feasted upon the rich

fare brought to them, and sold the silver dish and plates, on the produce of which they lived happily for some weeks. Aladdin was now able to dress well, and in taking his usual walk, he one day chanced to see the Sultan's daughter coming with her attendants from the baths. He was so much struck with her beauty, that he fell in love with her at once, and told his mother that she must go to the Sultan, and ask him to give the Princess to be his wife. The poor woman said he must be crazy; but her son not only knew what a treasure he had got in the Magic Lamp, but he had also found how valuable were the shining fruits he had gathered, which he thought at the time to be only coloured glass. At first he sent a bowlful of these jewels—for so they were—to the Sultan, who was amazed at their richness, and said to Aladdin's mother: "Your son shall have his wish, if he can send me, in a week, forty bowls like this, carried by twenty white and twenty black slaves, handsomely dressed." He thought by this to keep what he had got, and to hear no more of Aladdin. But the Genius of the Lamp soon brought the bowls of jewels and the slaves, and Aladdin's mother went with them to the Sultan.

The Sultan was overjoyed at receiving these rich gifts, and at once agreed that the Princess

Ring to help him, but all he could do was to take him to Africa. The Princess was rejoiced to see him again, but was very sorry to find that she had been the cause of all their trouble by parting with the wonderful Lamp. Aladdin, however, consoled her, and told her that he had thought of a plan for getting it back. He then left her, but soon returned with a powerful sleeping-draught, and advised her to receive the Magician with pretended kindness, and pour it into his wine at dinner that day, so as to make him fall sound asleep, when they could take the Lamp from him. Everything happened as they expected ; the Magician drank the wine, and when Aladdin came in, he found that he had fallen back lifeless on the couch. Aladdin took the Lamp from his bosom, and called upon the Genius to transport the Palace, the Princess, and himself, back to their native city. The Sultan was as much astonished and pleased at their return, as he had been provoked at the loss of his daughter ; and Aladdin, with his Bulbul, lived long afterwards to enjoy his good fortune.